The Tree
Nobody Wanted

A Christmas Story

The Tree
Nobody Wanted

A Christmas Story

Tom McCann

Exeter Press
B O S T O N

For information about permission to reproduce or transmit selections
from this book in any form or by any means, write to
EXETER PRESS BOSTON
223 Commonwealth Avenue, Boston MA 02116
tel: 617-267-7720
fax: 617-262-6948
www.exeterpress.com

Library of Congress Control Number: 2007931565
ISBN 978-0-9797407-0-1

Printed in the United States of America
First Edition

Special thanks to Frederick Jillson for his illustrations, Nan Fornal for
her editing, Skye Wentworth for her work as publicist, and
Jon Albertson for his design of this book.

For Joan

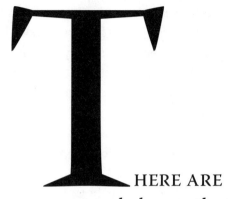

HERE ARE
things poor people know that
others do not. All kinds of things.
The list is very long, and I don't know
them all. But I do know some of
them. One thing poor people know
is that at eight o'clock on Christmas
Eve all over the world, the men who
sell Christmas trees simply walk off
their rented spaces and begin their
own Christmas celebrations. They
just leave behind the unsold
Christmas trees.

Some years there are a great many trees left; other years, just a few. After the sellers leave, people who didn't have enough money to buy a tree earlier pick over what is left. Some years they get a good tree; some years, a not-so-good tree; and some years they can't find a tree at all.

The year was 1946, one year after the end of World War II. The place was the Brownsville section of Brooklyn, where I was born eleven years earlier. It was a bad neighborhood when I lived there; it's a lot worse now. Some very poor people still live there, and there is more violence there now than there was in 1946. For reasons I'll explain later, I lived with my grandmother — my mother's mother — and our canary, Sweetie, in a two-room apartment on the third floor. We lived in what was called a cold-water flat because it had no hot water and no central heating. It was cold in winter and hot in summer. The "El," as the elevated train is called, passed within about twenty feet of our windows, and the riders looked into our apartment the same way we looked at them through the train windows as they passed by. There was a sharp curve in the tracks, so the engineer had to slow down as the train approached our windows, giving us and the riders a good look at each other. As the train rounded the

curve, the steel wheels strained against the steel tracks, making a loud screeching noise. When we first moved there, the noise kept us awake at night, but after a few weeks we no longer heard it, even with all the windows open in summer.

At about seven o'clock that Christmas Eve, Nanny — that's what I always called my grandmother — reminded me to get ready to go, so I'd be there early and have the best chance of getting a good tree. She reminded me, as she always did, to wear my heavy coat against the cold night air, to wear the woolen gloves she had made for me that past summer, and to pull my woolen hat down over my ears. Sometimes on really cold and windy days she stuffed a newspaper, usually the *Brooklyn Eagle*, inside my shirt. It kept me warm.

Christmas trees were sold on nearly every street corner in those days, but for some unknown reason I walked to the lot on the corner of Nostrand Avenue and Carroll Street even though there were some places closer to where we lived. I often think about how things would have been different if I had chosen another one of those lots. The lot I chose had only a few trees left, but something told me I would have good luck there. I waited on the other side of the street. At exactly eight o'clock, according to the clock outside the Dime Savings Bank, the bare light bulbs of the Christmas tree sellers started to go out one string at a time. When the last string of lights went out a minute later, three men walked away, all going in different directions.

I quickly crossed the street and looked at what they had left. There were only three trees. One was very tall and skinny and would not have fit in our apartment. The second tree was about seven feet tall. It would have fit, but it was very full and wasn't shaped like a Christmas tree. It was square, not tapered. If Nan had seen that one, she would have said something like, "With some work, that one will do," as she was fond of saying about things that were barely adequate. The third tree did not look like a tree at all. It was about as tall as I was, about five feet, but had hardly any branches. In fact, one side was completely bare of branches, and it was missing that most important branch — the one that pointed straight up, the one to which the star or the angel was attached. Actually, the star was one of the few real ornaments we had. If I took this tree, there would be no place to attach the star. I remember thinking I could find a way to get the star to stay at the top, and we could always face the flat side of the tree to the wall. I could have taken the second tree and shaped it with Nan's carving knife. Or I could have taken the tall, skinny one and borrowed a saw from someone and cut a few feet off the top of it. But there was something about this small, ugly — yes, it was ugly — misshapen tree that made me choose it, and so I did.

I told myself there were a lot of really good things about the tree. It smelled so good, like fresh pine! It was also a beautiful green. It was small and wouldn't need a lot of ornaments to cover it. That was good. Another really good thing about this tree, I told myself, was that it was small enough for me to carry. I would have had to drag home either of the others, and it would lose a lot of needles off the branches along the way.

As I carried the little tree under my arm, occasionally having to shift it from arm to arm, I began to wonder what kind of a life it had before it was cut down. I wondered where it came from — Nova Scotia or somewhere else in Canada, perhaps, or possibly Vermont. All of those places were very far away from Brooklyn. I began to think of the sadness of its being cut down long before it had a chance to grow up to its full height. I wondered why the man who cut it down

chose it. It certainly was not a tree anyone would buy. The proof of that was it was left unsold. Nobody wanted it. I began to think what it must have been like for the tree to have been cut down…tied up with a piece of rope…thrown on a truck…moved to a city…been looked at and then rejected by so many people for the past month. What it must have felt like when those lights went out on the lot, not knowing what was going to happen the day after Christmas. I knew what happened to Christmas trees after they served their purpose: They were put out for the garbage trucks and would end up in the city dump. And the city dump was a terrible place. Those were just some of my thoughts on the way home. I was beginning to think of the tree in human terms. I knew that was silly, but I couldn't help it.

I had no trouble getting the tree up the three flights of stairs. I could see by the fleeting look on Nanny's face that she was disappointed. "Where are we going to hang the star?" she asked and went on, "It is very one-sided…it seems crooked." I had answers for all of her comments, which were as mild as everything else about her. Nanny never strenuously objected to anything and was always forgiving and understanding. That was one of the things I loved most about her and

marveled at, especially since life had dealt her some severe blows.

After a few minutes, she smiled and said, "This little tree will do nicely, but we have to figure out a way to get the star on top." So I first wired a stick to the trunk and then the star to the stick. It was perfect. Next, I placed the tree in the corner of the room with the flat, bare side facing the wall. As soon as I had it placed, Sweetie, whose cage door was always open, flew to the top of the tree and sang a song Nanny and I had never before heard. She had never been in a tree, and she loved it. It was beginning to look like a Christmas tree.

Nan made us a cup of tea and took out a tin box of shortbread cookies. She lighted the two red candles she held over from year to year. She talked about things past. She started by telling me the story of the first Christmas, which I had heard dozens of times but never tired of hearing. She told me stories about my mother, her only daughter, who died giving birth to me and my twin brother. Despite the fact that he was still-born, he was given the name James, and I was named Thomas, which I was told means "the twin" in Greek. I asked Nanny about my father, and she repeated what she always told me: She said she never knew him or anything about him. She said she never knew who he was, what he was, or where he came from. He was a mystery my mother took to the grave with her. I asked Nan if she thought one of us was named for him, and she said she was sure we were not. She said my mother picked out those names before we were born, as soon as the doctor at the clinic told her she was having twins. Then Nan said something that has stayed with me all my life. She said that my mother told her that she would not name any babies after him and that she had no intention of giving her twins his name. Nan said I should respect my mother's wishes and not ever look for him, that I should accept what was written on my birth certificate in the father line —"unknown."

Then she abruptly changed the subject. We never again talked about my father, and I have never looked for him.

We continued to talk about Nan's life, about her mother and father and about the older man she married at the age of fifteen just to get out of her house and away from her strict and mean mother. Her mother made young Nanny do all the housework and the raising of the other seven children. We talked about the future. She always said that she hoped she would live long enough to see me become eighteen, an age at which I could take care of myself. That kind of talk always frightened me and made me sad. I could not imagine a life without Nanny. Nan's two sons, my uncles Arthur and Charles, helped us out as much as they could with money and groceries and in other ways, especially Uncle Arthur. In three years Uncle Charlie would be dead of his alcoholism, and Nanny would bury another one of her children.

Suddenly, I felt very tired, probably from carrying the tree so far. Nanny suggested I lie down on the sofa "just for a few minutes."

I closed my eyes and thought of past Christmas Eves. It was the most exciting night of the year. I would lie in bed for hours with visions of Santa Claus streaking across the cold, moonlit sky in his sled loaded with presents, pulled by eight beautiful white reindeer. I used to think I could actually hear the bells on his sleigh and the clunk as he landed on the rooftop. We did not have a chimney for him to climb down or a fireplace to hang stockings, but Nanny would leave the door unlocked for him. He would leave presents for me and then be on his way to the next house, where he would climb down the chimney, fill the stockings left hanging near the fireplace, spread the gifts under the Christmas tree, and take off for the next house.

The last thing I remember after closing my eyes was the sound of Nanny striking a match to light the kerosene stove. The warm air from the stove filled the room, and in a minute or two I was asleep.

When I woke up, it was the next morning, Christmas! I was still on the sofa under a woolen blanket that Nanny had knitted and with a pillow under my head. The first thing I saw was the tree. I couldn't believe it. It was beautiful. I'll never forget that first sight of it. There were just five or six ornaments on it. No lights, and no presents under it, of course. But hanging on every branch were the things that Nan and

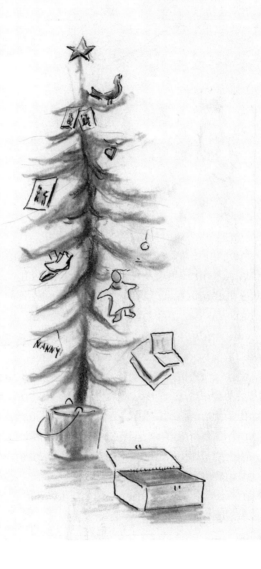

I cherished. We kept them in a large tin box, and we always said that if we ever had a fire, all we had to take was that one box. Everything in the world that was dear to us was on that tree. There were the two pictures of my mother — Nanny's daughter — one taken when she was a schoolgirl and the other taken a month or so before she died. It was my favorite picture because I could see that she was carrying my brother and me, and that made me feel very close to her and to him. On another branch was the heart-shaped locket she was wearing when she died. It opened up, and on one side was a tiny picture of Nan. The other side was empty. Nan was all my mother had in life, just as, eleven years later, Nanny was all I had in life.

On another branch there were pictures of Nanny as a young girl and as a bride at fifteen, standing next to a man more than twice her age — her husband — whom she would call "Mr. Phillips" for the next twelve years until he died, leaving her a twenty-seven-year-old widow with three children. There were also pictures of her father, Lincoln Alexander, so named because he was born on April 14, 1865, the night Abraham Lincoln was shot. Nanny loved her father. She would often say that he was gentle and kind and worked hard every day of his life. There were no pictures of her mother, a cold, stern, unhappy woman, who came to this country from Germany before World War I and who thought that everything in America was inferior to everything in Germany. She longed to go back to her country but never did.

Hanging from one of the stronger lower branches was a small doll that had belonged to my mother. Above that, my mother's first pair of baby shoes. And hanging from a white ribbon was a tiny ring that was given to her when she was a baby — a gift from a Catholic nun who worked as a nurse in the hospital where my mother had been born. Sister Miriam was her name, and she told Nanny the ring had been hers when she was a baby. She had been waiting to give it to a baby whose name was Miriam. That was the name Nanny had given my mother the day she was born.

Hanging from other branches were letters my mother had written to Nanny as a child, telling her the kinds of things kids tell their mothers. There was also a first-prize medal she had won in an ASPCA "Be Kind to Animals" drawing contest. Nanny said my mother was a very good artist, but we did not have any of her drawings.

From other branches were hung notes from me to Nan, written in my early, childish writing, with poor spelling and limited vocabulary. Also hanging on the

tree were little art objects I had made for her at school, including a pin spelling out "Nanny" in alphabet macaroni mounted on half a popsicle stick with a pin glued onto the back. The stick was stained brown with shoe polish, and the letters painted gold. Nanny loved it and wore it from time to time, and now it was on our tree with her other cherished things.

These things on our homely little Christmas tree transformed it into a personal, meaningful, colorful, and beautiful work of art, at least to Nanny and me. I doubt that anyone else would have seen it that way, but it didn't matter because that's what it was to us.

Nanny watched me as I examined every branch. I ran to her and held her close. "I'm glad you like what we have done with your little tree. I'm so glad you picked that tree," she said.

"I love it, Nan, and I love you," I managed to say.

"And I love you, too, Thomas. I know that sometimes I am a little stern with you, but that's only because I want you to grow up to be a good, strong man who will someday be a good husband, father, and even grandfather. I'll be gone, but I'll be looking down on you and smiling just as I am now. Sometimes I get a little angry that I can't give you a better life, but I do the best I can and I think you know that. You don't have what a lot of the other boys have, like bicycles and baseball gloves, but . . ." Her voice trailed off. "Maybe next year we'll have something to put under the tree," she said.

For a long time we just sat there holding hands and looking at our magnificent Christmas tree. There were no lights on it, and few ornaments, but it glistened as though it were bathed in light and colors. It was magical.

After a while Nanny sent me to the live-chicken market on Atlantic Avenue for a fresh-killed 25-cent chicken for our Christmas dinner.

I didn't want that Christmas Day to end, but, like all days, it did. Soon it was the weekend and our tree was starting to show signs of drying out. The needles began falling to the floor, and the branches began to droop. I dreaded what I would soon have to do.

I told Nanny I couldn't bear the thought of putting it out for the sanitation men to pick up and throw on a pile of other trees and then throw other trees onto our little tree and crush the life out of it. The next day, Nanny took everything off the tree and put things back in the tin box, leaving the little tree in almost the same condition it was in when I brought it home except for the drooping branches and falling needles. "You'll find a proper place for it…you'll see," she said. As I gathered the tree in my arms, Nan gently touched two of its branches, and I could see a tear roll down her cheek. Sweetie stopped singing and returned to her cage as I walked out the door of our tiny apartment.

Outside with the tree under my arm once again, I remember not knowing which way to go. A voice inside me told me to make a left turn, which put me on Fulton Street. Next, something told me to take another left onto Utica Avenue, and from there a right onto Eastern Parkway. I began to see signs pointing the way to the Brooklyn Botanic Garden. Soon, I was in front of its stately granite entrance. The Botanic Garden occupies a large part of Brooklyn's beautiful Prospect Park. It was Sunday so the heavy iron gates were open, but there were no employees around and few other people. It had snowed the night before.

I entered the garden and began to walk its snow-covered paths. Suddenly, in front of me was a grove of pine trees. Some were tall, and others were as short as my little tree. Once again, that voice inside me — the same one that led me to my tree on Christmas Eve — told me that this was the place I should leave my tree, where it would be surrounded by other trees and plants and flowers. I looked around and saw a stone building that I assumed was a tool shed. It was open, and I walked in and selected a sharp, pointy shovel. I began to dig in the center of the pine grove. But the ground was frozen solid. Returning to the tool shed, I found a heavy iron bar about six feet long, and after about an hour I had managed to dig a hole only eight inches deep, just big enough around to fit the base of the tree into the ground, but not deep enough to enable it to stand by itself. I found a few stones in the shed and put them around the base. I packed some freshly fallen snow around the stones. Our little tree was standing straight, and to me it looked as though it belonged there. I stood there in front of it for what was probably a long time thinking words of good-bye. When I could no longer feel my feet from the cold, I walked away, looking back over my shoulder until I could no longer see Nanny's and my tree.

I knew it wouldn't grow. It had no roots to nourish it with water and things from the soil that made trees grow. I knew it would fall over eventually, or some Botanic Garden worker would pull it out of the shallow hole, recognizing that it was not one of their own healthy and beautiful specimens. I didn't want to think what he might do with it. At least the tree was standing now and was among other trees if only for a brief time.

That January set a new record for snowfall: It snowed almost every day. Nanny got pneumonia and was too weak to get out of bed most of the month. Her illness frightened me. She was all I had, and I loved her so much. I did the washing of our clothes, and from her sickbed Nan taught me how to cook her favorite chicken soup, which was all she wanted to eat. Uncle Arthur brought us food and medicine for her cough and repaired the kerosene stove within hours of its breaking down. Nanny recovered. My prayers were answered.

In February I visited the pine grove at the Botanic Garden where I had left our tree. To my surprise, it was still there. Still standing. There had been more snow, and it had frozen over and provided the additional support the tree needed to stand upright. Again, I stood in front of it and probably even spoke to it. I know before I left that day I reached out and touched it just as Nanny had done the day I took it out of our apartment.

On my birthday, March 8th, which was also the day my mother and baby brother had died and was always a very sad day for me, I went to the Garden once again, and the tree had still not fallen or been moved. A month later, on Easter Sunday, I went back. The snow was melting, but the tree was still standing. As I got closer, I noticed that the branches were no longer drooping and no needles had fallen off. I assumed that some moisture had gotten up to the branches through the trunk, but I knew it was only temporary and that my tree without roots could not live.

A month later, in May, I saw new, light-green growth sprouting out from the trunk at the bottom of the tree. By June there were more new sprouts reaching toward the top. There was a chirping sound coming from a bird's nest. I could see the heads of the baby birds peeking out of the nest; soon they were flying under the watchful eye of their mother. By the end of the summer the sprouts of early spring had turned into

new branches — not very sturdy, but branches — and they were filling in the back of the tree, which had been flat and bare at Christmastime. The birds had left the nest, gone to live their lives in other trees and in other places, as birds do.

By the following Christmas I was certain that my tree was alive. It seemed to me that it had grown about a foot since I had planted it, and filled out on the sides as well.

I told all of this to Nanny each time I visited the Botanic Garden. She smiled and told me how wonderful it was, but behind her smile I could see doubt. On Memorial Day we always visited "the graves," which were in Brooklyn and Queens. Uncle Arthur had a '36 Plymouth and took us to visit all the people in our family we had buried there. We placed flowers and a small flag on each grave and said a prayer as we looked at the names on the gravestones. It was always quiet in the car on the way back from visiting the last of the graves.

This time, though, Nanny broke the silence and asked Uncle Arthur to drive us to the Botanic Garden. What she saw when we got there was what I had described to her. Our tree had grown more than a foot, sprouted new branches, and was filled in all around, healthy and a vibrant green. She went over to it, and I thought I heard her say a few words, but I couldn't be sure because Uncle Arthur and I were standing back a bit to give her room to be alone with our tree. After a few minutes she once again gently touched its branches as she turned away. Back in the car, Nanny turned to me and said, "I owe you an apology, Thomas. I didn't believe what you said about our tree coming back to life. I do now."

In the years ahead I visited the tree often. I never missed a year. Each time I did I felt a kind of presence… a bond between the tree and me that seemed to grow stronger as the years passed. I felt that somehow it remembered that Christmas Day long ago. In fact, I felt it remembered all of its history both before and after we met in that darkened lot on the corner of Nostrand and Carroll. On my visits I would bring the tree up to date, telling it of the many twists and turns my life had taken. One year — it was 1972 — I had to tell it the sad news that Nanny had passed on a month earlier. At that moment, on what had been a calm summer day, a strong, cold wind came suddenly, and the tree swayed and twisted to one side as a person would turn away

to avert revealing facial expression in an emotional moment. I knew the tree had understood the sad news I brought it that day.

One day a short time later I visited the tree and was surprised to find that a twelve-inch brass sign had been placed in the ground in front of it. On it was engraved

BALSAM FIR (Pinus balsamnea)

Native to the northeastern United States. Its soft, fragrant foliage makes it prized as a Christmas tree. This perfect specimen was left at the Brooklyn Botanic Garden in December 1946 by an anonymous donor.

Balsam firs have been known to reach a height of more than ninety (90) feet. The oldest recorded specimen, based on tree-ring chronology, had reached 245 years when it was collected at Lac Liberal, Canada.

At last, our little tree had a name; it will grow taller and older…much older. And, best of all, according to the sign, it is a "perfect specimen." That day was one of the best days of my life.

Sixty years have passed since that Christmas Day in 1946. I live in Boston now, and I don't get to New York very often. There really is no reason for me to go there. All my relatives are gone. Our tree is my only living connection to Brooklyn and New York. I think about our tree a lot and wonder how it was that it came back to life. Several years ago, I met a professor of botany at one of Boston's great universities. I told him the story, thinking it would interest him and hoping he might be able to explain how it might happen that a tree with no roots could come back to life and still be growing after all these years. The professor told me that under certain conditions it is possible for a tree that was cut off at ground level to take up nourishment through other means and to grow new roots. He said the process is similar to the growing of tomatoes and other fruits and vegetables hydroponically. I'm sure he is right, but I prefer to think there was some other force at work that restored our beloved little Christmas tree, that brought it back to life, has kept it alive, and will continue to keep it alive. Nan's and my tree is well over thirty feet tall today, and it is still growing.

One day last winter, I was flying into New York. I noticed that the plane took an unusual path down the west side of Manhattan along the Hudson River, past the site of what used to be the World Trade Center. At the tip of Manhattan I could see Battery Park — where the Staten Island Ferry comes in — and, just offshore, the Statue of Liberty. The pilot banked sharply left, which took us over Brooklyn on our way to Kennedy airport. As I looked down, I saw that we were flying directly over Prospect Park and the Brooklyn Botanic Garden. For an instant I thought I could actually see our Christmas tree, but I can't be sure because at that moment the pilot banked the plane again to head toward JFK. We were flying very low, and I could see the corner of Nostrand and Carroll and the approximate place where our apartment was. I could see Brownsville, where I was born and where my mother and brother died, my grammar school, my high school in Queens, and so many other familiar landmarks of the places where I spent the first twenty years of my life. Off to the left, in the distance, I saw the cemeteries we visited every Memorial Day, where so many of our family are buried, including Nanny. As the plane slowed and sank lower over Jamaica Bay, my thoughts went back to our tree. At the moment the wheels touched down on the runway, I knew I was not going to make my connection to Los Angeles that day.

I left my luggage with the airline's baggage department, and minutes later I was in a taxi headed for Brooklyn and my old neighborhood.

T HE APARTMENT BUILDING where Nanny and I lived was still there. It looked pretty much the same except for iron bars on the windows of the lower floors and an ugly gray steel door, with heavy-duty locks, at the front. I had an urge to ring the bell of apartment 3A and tell the person who answered over the intercom my name and that I used to live there, and ask if I could go in and just look around. I didn't. Instead, I decided to walk the neighborhood.

The live-chicken market on Atlantic Avenue was gone, and in its place was a bodega. Jack's Candy Store, where my friends and I all spent so much time and so little money, was also gone. I wondered what happened to Jack Edelstein — a good man who let us come into his little store to get warm despite the fact that we seldom bought anything. Roitman's Drug Store was gone, too, its building now home to a check-cashing store, something we never had when I was growing up. There were no checks then. Men got paid in cash in little yellow envelopes, and people paid for what they bought with that cash. There weren't any credit cards in those days, either. The Earl Theater — always a double feature, three cartoons, and Movietone News, all for twelve cents — was gone and was now a variety bargain store. Schembri's Fruit Store, where for five cents you could get enough "soup greens" to make a big pot of stew, was now vacant and all boarded up. Zeiler's Kosher Butcher Shop was still a meat market, but I knew by the dozens of skinned and unskinned rabbits in the window that it was no longer a kosher market. Temple Beth Zion was now a Pentecostal church with badly done imitation stained glass windows of Jesus and his Apostles. A few things remained: St. Michael's Catholic Church was there, and so was Christ Lutheran, but a pile of stiff, yellowed newspapers piled against the door gave the impression that the church was no longer used very much. A new Russian church stood where some other church had been. The site of Liberty Hospital, where I was born and where my mother and brother had died, was now a large cinema complex with a marquee boasting of ten screens. Its walls were covered in spray-paint graffiti. When I was a boy, I used to walk around the hospital and look at it, trying to visualize the scene inside on the night I was born. Now it is a movie theater. Goldstein's pickle factory was gone...the El was moved underground in the fifties. The Savarin Coffee Company was gone, too, and with it the aroma of freshly ground coffee — thousands of pounds of it each day — that filled our neighborhood.

Gone, too, was Ebbets Field, home of the Brooklyn Dodgers, where Uncle Arthur and I would sit in the bleachers and thrill to the plays of Jackie Robinson, Pee Wee Reese, Gil Hodges, Duke Snider, and Carl Furillo of the accurate rifle-fire arm. I began walking in the direction of Nostrand Avenue and Carroll Street, where I'd found the tree and chosen it over the others that were passed over and abandoned. The lot was now home to a bar called Club 880. Across the street used to be the exclusive Jesuit high school, Brooklyn Prep. It's now Medgar Evers Junior College, named after the man who was known for his struggles for civil rights in Mississippi and who was killed by an assassin.

Soon it would be dark, and this was not a neighborhood for a stranger to be in at night. That was true even when I lived there, and it is especially true now. It was also getting colder, a lot like those nights so long ago when I went out in search of a Christmas tree and Nanny had made me put a newspaper inside my shirt to help keep me warm. I went into a bodega and bought a newspaper and then unbuttoned my shirt and slipped it inside as Nanny had taught me to do. It was so cold that there weren't many people on the street. Those that were looked nothing like the people from my old neighborhood. There were people in turbans, Middle Eastern headgear, colorful satin team jackets, baseball caps turned backwards, Nike running shoes. Many of them were listening to music on headsets or talking on cell phones. My old neighborhood had been replaced by a new one, with new people from different lands: India, Haiti, Russia, Vietnam, Colombia, Lebanon, Puerto Rico, and others. Only a few things remained from the old neighborhood — a very few things.

I quickly headed up Fulton Street. I took a left on Utica Avenue and then a right on Eastern Parkway. Suddenly, I was at the same stately granite entrance of the Brooklyn Botanic Garden. It had not changed since the day I took our tree there. Once again, the gates were open, and I went directly to the grove of pine trees and stood in front of our tree, Nanny's and mine. It had a life with us. And I know it had a full life after it left us, including a near-miraculous rebirth. It had a life in this garden with the other trees and plants and flowers and the thousands upon thousands of people who passed in front of it and admired its beauty and strength. I knew our tree would go on living long after I am gone, but I also knew it would remember me as long as it lived. I believe that all living things have feelings and memory.

Darkness comes early in winter, and it was approaching very fast. I said good-bye to our tree, perhaps for the last time, and I sensed a sadness coming from it. I reached out and gently touched a branch, the way Nanny used to do, and a piece of it came off in my hand. I put it in my coat pocket and said good-bye one more time. I turned and walked out of the Botanic Garden and across the wide street. As I reached the corner, I turned for one last look at our tree because I realized that once I turned the corner I would no longer be able to see it. Life is many things, including a series of turning corners. One minute things are in front of you in full view, and the next instant you can no longer see what was there. All you have left is the memory. All I have of our tree now is the memory of it and the piece of the broken branch it gave to me. Later that night, I returned to JFK and boarded a flight to Los Angeles.

A few days later on the plane coming back to Boston, I decided to write this story in the hope that someday my children, perhaps with their own children, will visit Nanny's and my Christmas tree. I hope they will see it and know that it is a living link with the past of their father and his much-loved Nanny, and many other relatives known and unknown.

Tom McCann is the author of the critically acclaimed best-selling nonfiction book *An American Company: The Tragedy of United Fruit* (Crown, 1976) and the novel *Earth Angel*, published in 2002. He is also a playwright and has written several screen- and teleplays. McCann is a television producer who has produced prime-time docudramas for both network and public television. He was born in Brooklyn and now lives in Boston.